To my family who walked with me a while

NOTE: THESE ACTIVITIES ARE MEANT TO BE WITH ADULT PERMISSION, SUPERVISION AND RESPONSIBILITY.

Walk With Me A While is a children's book of the nostalgic wonder of childhood moments. Here are some excerpts. Walk with me a while, find materials to create. Turn a paper into a mask and bed sheet into a cape. Walk with me a while, look for the art on the rocks and leaves like treasures waiting to be found.

Walk With Me A While©Marites Castro Jan 2021

TABLE OF CONTENTS

FALLING LEAVES

Walk with me a while, see the changing colors and hear the gentle sound of the falling leaves.

RAINDROPS

Walk with me a while, eat ice cream in the light summer rain. Feel the raindrops on your gentle face.

BUNNY

Walk with me a while, hand out flyers about a lost bunny. Weeks later, what was lost was now found!

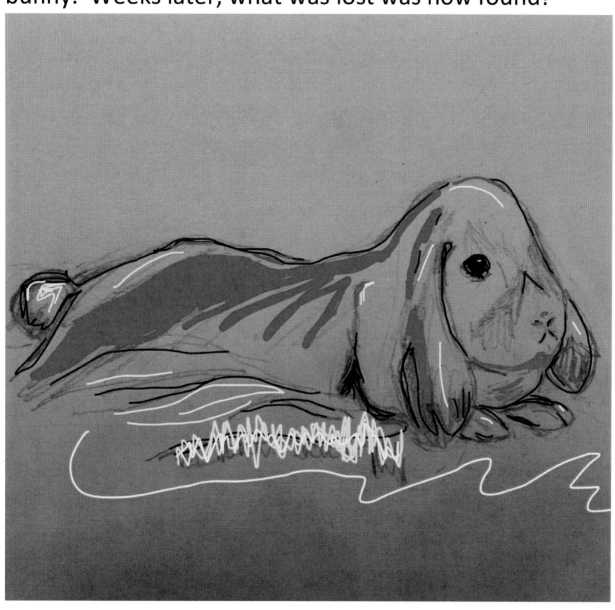

BIRD

Walk with me a while, hear the bird singing in early spring.

TREES

Walk with me a while, say hello to the trees gently waving and sparkling their leaves to people walking by.

SWEETS

Walk with me a while, taste some lollipops to bring sweetness and a little smile.

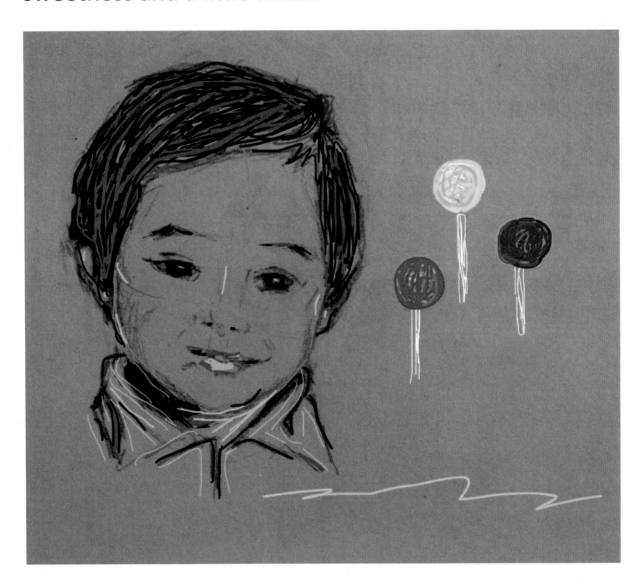

FLOWERS

Walk with me a while, cut some fresh flowers from the garden for an elderly neighbor nearby.

FOOD

Walk with me a while, raise money to give delicious food for the hungry.

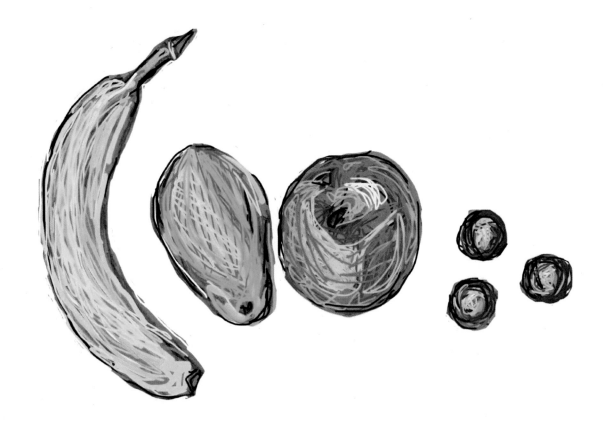

PIER

Walk with me a while, look over the pier. Enjoy the sparkling ocean and go fishing for fun.

SNOW

Walk with me a while, feel the crisp air and stand in wonder of the frozen icicles and snow.

SCHOOL BUS

Walk with me a while, wait for the school bus in the rain, shine, or snow.

DRAGONFLIES

Walk with me a while, search for the dragonflies and butterflies flying among the flowers and trees.

ROLL DOWN

Walk with me a while, roll down a gentle sloping mound in the park. Fill the summer air with laughter of pure delight and thrill.

BEACH

Walk with me a while, touch the sand, ocean, starfish and sea shells all around.

TREASURES

Walk with me a while, look for the art on the rocks and leaves like treasures waiting to be found.

SUPER HEROES

Walk with me a while, find materials to create. Turn a paper into a mask and bed sheet into a cape.

LAKE

Walk with me a while, watch the sail and walk the trails around the lake.

QUIET MOMENTS

Walk with me a while, find a place to slow down and quiet the heart and mind.

MEMORIES

Walk with me a while, visit family to create memories and leave footprints behind.

LONG WAY HOME

Walk with me a while, laugh and imagine the adventures of different paths on the long way home.

Made in the USA
Monee, IL
25 March 2023

30062427R00017